The Book-lover
And
The Football-fan

The Book-lover And The Football-fan

A novel about Very and Brian

Copyright Henrik Neergaard 2020

Published by: Books-on-Demand. Copenhagen, Denmark

Printed by: Books-on-Demand, Norderstedt, Germany

ISBN: 9788743026822

Henrik Neergaard

The Book-lover And The Football-fan

A novel about Vera and Brian

Books-on-Demand

Some other books by Henrik Neergaard,

Published by Books-on-Demand

My nightly wanderings under shining stars and darken sky.

A novel

The serpent and the forbidden fruit.

And other short stories

A real big beer

It was a little bit changing weather. That was to be noted. Right now it was cloudy. Earlier in the day it had been sunshine. At least for periods. Short periods. Grey weather, too. Same thing earlier in the day. For several rounds. In between periods of sunshine. It changed all the time. It also blew quite a bit.

It was mid-April, but it did not like it was spring, even if the season was for it. Rather like autumn weather, Vera noted, and sighed. She did not like autumn weather very much, but on the other hand she loved the sun and summer. And at least a little bit of spring.

"At that point you're probably fairly normal," Brian noted with that little grin that had become so characteristic of him over the years. It was one of his favorite remarks. He had more sayings like that, but this was one of the ones he used really often. "At that point, you're probably fairly normal." He said that a lot. Not just to Vera, but also to all sorts of others.

But of most of all to Vera, his wife through almost quite a few years now. To her, he said it almost all the time. At least several times a day when she commented on one and the other and spread about what she liked and what she did not like. But he also said it happy and happy to the family's other members, and to whom he otherwise met on his way and fell in love with. Because he did. Fell in conversation with people he met. Even if it was someone he did not know very well, or maybe did not even know.

He liked to get a little chat with people. A nice little thing, as he called it, like a little beer or two. That was the term he used. A little beer, it was a regular beer. A hawker's beer. For his sake like the cheap ones from the supermarket. They tasted almost as good, he said. It was not something he cared about very much.

A giant was a gold beer.

"Are we going to have a beer?" one of his acquaintances asked.

"Yes, let's take one of the slightly bigger ones today," he might say. Especially if it was the other's turn to give.

But, of course, it was not the whole register he had to play on. A real giant was an elephant beer or something similar. But about elephant beers, he had a particular weakness for those. It was his favorite. Then he could be blissful.

"That was what deserves a really big beer!" he might say, if he had been excited about something. For example, it could be a particularly good or particularly important goal in a football match. But of course only if it was the right team that had scored. That goes without saying. If, for example, it was Denmark that had scored in a national match. And of course, most if it was not just a friendly match, but a fight that mattered. Then the Real Big Beers sat loose with him. Then he suddenly became generous and passed out right and left to everyone who was nearby, whether he knew them or not.

It was Vera, his wife, not very excited about. Because they also had to think about the household budget, as she said. Such a European Championship or World Cup, where Denmark were in, and perhaps even reached the quarter-finals, it could well drain their household budget so much that they almost had to live on water porridge the whole of the following month. At least, if you were to believe her interpretation of it, not everyone did. And least of all of course Brian. But on the other hand, it was not something that particularly challenged him. He did not want to spend energy on things like that, he said. And so there was never really that argument or discussion about what Vera had probably been hoping for.

For it was probably really about her being jealous of his great football interest during such a period when he was not interested in much other than the matches on TV. And not for her either. She often complained that he neglected her in favor of football. It was almost as bad as if he had had a real mistress of flesh and blood, she said.

But I don't think she really meant that anyway. It was just something she said. I'm pretty sure she would have taken even more on the road if he had had a real mistress. And that is understandable. So it's probably very good that she did not know anything about the little affairs he had had around the hooks.

But his footballing interest, she was jealous of that. For lack of better, as Jeanette used to say. But in a way, it was really quite practical, and quite clever, because all the football stuff caught all her attention. Apparently, it covered her need to be jealous. That was how it actually worked. You could almost have called it a diversion, that is, from his side, to dispel her interest in everything else he was doing, which she could be jealous of for at least as much reason. Or for even better reason, actually. If it had been a deliberate technique he used to divert her attention from everything else- but I'm pretty sure it was not. It was just because he loved football so much.

But nonetheless, Vera felt bypassed in those situations. And it was not just when there was the World Cup or the European Championships. It was his footballing interest as such that she was mad at. But it was of course the worst if it was one of the big tournaments, and especially if Denmark was in it. Whether it was justified or not. For so much money, he could not, after all, drain the household budget, although it must be admitted that he was generous with the elephant bees for such a period of time, which many of us unreservedly benefited from.

And it is also true that he initially pretended that the thing with porridge day after day did not challenge him at all, but it just did not last long.

A week maybe, or barely 14 days, when he pretended to be completely indifferent to that, but then no more. Then he gradually began to gripe about it, and more and more, for each day that passed. And the last week of such a water porridge month, he was vinegary every day for dinner time, and by the way, the rest of the day. It was a nuisance to be near him when he was like that. There was not what he could not think of.

But once this time of trials was over, Vera used to celebrate the end of the fasting month with a proper game of pork roast with browned potatoes and white potatoes and red cabbage and sour and currant jelly and oceans of bold brown pork sauce, which, incidentally, she was a true master of making in just the right way. And when the day of this feast came to an end – far outside the Christmas season – it was as if Brian was alive again and forgave her the previous month's heavy afflictions. So now all of a sudden everything was back as before. At least that was how it worked.

So Vera apparently belonged to the slightly older generation of women who are convinced that the way to man's heart goes through the stomach. And something could indicate that she was right, at least in this case. So, of course, she understood how to exploit that. First to punish him for his footballing passion and his enthusiasm for the easy-flowing elephants and all the many full- and half-full football and elephant fans he dragged home or generously invited on that occasion. And then in the second, by marking that now the punishment was over for this time, by serving the sumptuous pork roast dinner, where she had often made so plentiful that it stretched to three or four days.

But only then did he just have to be punished with a month on water porridge. And almost as spartan and scraped breakfast and lunch, that was part of the story. For there were three things she could not stand: football, drowning men and a spouse who, as a result of her solidarity with the first two factors, was lost to the outside world and, in particular, to her.

Self-development

It was an evening just over mid-April. Spring had, in between, made small tentative approaches to beautify the daily lives of optimists -but it had not yet established itself on a more serious basis.

It had become a bit warmer in the weather, and it was good enough, but on the other hand it had been raining all day. And the really heavy and massive rain, where you absolutely preferred not to venture out unless you simply had to for some reason.

Unfortunately, this was just the way it was, Vera noted, because she was one of the unfortunate bastards who had had to move into it.

But that was the way it was.

Everything had its price.

Just like in the old days when she worked in the small basement shop with Bettina. They had had so many grand plans back then. And then it was all littered, even though they had worked like little horses to make it run around. It was much harder to run such a shop than they had imagined before they started. After all, none of them had any experience of it beforehand. But ideas and visions they had had plenty of.

It had been some tough few years. They had almost been dogged by bad luck, she thought. And still had to contend with a debt several years later. But that was many years ago now. Fortunately. Very many years ago. Back when they were young, Bettina and her. Before she met Brian, who actually helped save her from it, that was at least financially. That was so long ago. It was past now, it had been for decades. So she did not have to worry about that now.

But everything had its price. That is generally speaking. I don't think that was a thing that was left out of it. It was one of the things she had learned from it.

There is no free lunch, as the Americans say. It was Kenneth, her eldest, who had taught her that, and some other American words and phrases that they used over there. He still lived there. And still without a family. Completely preoccupied with his career. I think it went okay. Or significantly more than just okay, actually. But shouldn't he soon find himself a nice girl to marry and start a family with? But that was how all mothers feel, if their adults take a little while, she knew that.

That was just the way it was.

A little too much, she sometimes thought.

There's no such thing as a free lunch. Or other meals, for that matter. Unless you were a really cunning and clever thief who could steal himself for it without getting caught. Maybe some people got away with that, for a while, at least. But it had to be hugely strenuous, she thought. Then she had rather pay for her lunch herself.

Otherwise, there was always some kind of price to be paid for that lunch. Or whatever it was, I think it was almost about everything. There was always a price to be paid in return. Sooner or later.

Sometimes you could choose whether to save first and pay in advance, or if you wanted to wait and pay later.

And then you might have thought you'd got it for free, but you just did not have it anyway. It did not last long. Sooner or later, there was a bill to be paid. So you got rid of your debt and things got balanced again.

Or as Johnny said. That hunter. Brian's half-brother. Johnny was an incarnate hunter. Unlike Brian, who was not interested in that kind of thing. The only kind of outdoor life that interested him was to sit out in the garden and enjoy the good weather in the summer.

But Johnny, on the other hand. He went hunting with the local hunting club several times a week during the hunting season.

And Johnny had his own way of saying things. He used very often expressions and metaphors from his familiar hunting world. And it could have its own charm, she thought.

So here, too. She liked the way he said that. As when, for example, he dryly observed that you can't even fire a gun without a recoil. In that usual way, as he often said things.

It was his way of explaining it, really masculine and not to misunderstand. Basically, it was the same thing they meant. Of course he knew that. She was sure of that. He was not stupid.

Vera often had such periods when she cultivated such a thing with self-development. That was the way in slightly different versions. She had been through a few of them gradually. She had been to some courses of that kind. And read a lot of books and magazines. In the winter, she often went to lectures on such topics. It was mostly during the winter season that she really cultivated it, in the more theoretical way, that is.

In the summer, however, she used to say, she usually did it in real life.

To live in the present, and all that stuff. At least much more than in winter. And maybe a little more than Brian, she thought.

She could not entice him to do something like that. He did not want lectures or courses. It was not too bad, she thought.

She thought he would benefit from getting into that kind of thing. He could just start by reading a few books about it, maybe. In fact, she had suggested that to him several times.

But no, that kind of thing was not for him, he said. Sometimes it almost seemed like he was actually taking pride in being against all that and just dismissing it as nonsense and nonsense.

Then she had to go alone. And so she did. Throughout the winter. She had been doing this for a number of years.

It was not too much said that this was often what gave her meaning and content in life throughout the long and sour Danish winter through.

There were many other people looking for these courses, and of course there were many other people looking for these courses, although not getting as close to each other there as you often got at the weekend courses – and even more so if it was a internate course where she was away from home for a whole week. Some of her best friends she had had like that.

The speakers were usually very inspiring, not only because of what they were talking about, but also because of their personality. Some of them were really charismatic, so it beamed out of them how well you would get it if only you followed their instructions. Often in a way that it was clear from their body language and all that indefinable, which could sometimes almost knock her legs away from her – in the good way that is.

Ornamental clouds

Vera went outside, into the garden and to the garbage can with the garbage bag from the kitchen. It was around noon. There was now only about 15 minutes missing until the noon bell fell, and now it was starting to blow up.

The sun was still shining, as it had been doing ever since this morning, and it was really summery. But it was already blowing considerably more strongly than it had done earlier this morning. Maybe today it was a thunderstorm, she thought.

There was now no trace of grey thunderclouds however, or, for that matter, any clouds anywhere in the clear blue sky that were only disfigured by the mucous clouds of a few small and all-whites – of the kind that look like little white cotton s wool. What's more, there were exactly three long, long, white stripes from the Air Force jet fighters. These white stripes stretched across the entire sky, from horizon to horizon.

Or it was, in fact, a slightly wrong expression, what she had used in her thoughts and quiet mind, she thought. Imprecise, at least. Or just incorrect. In other words, not with beautiful weather clouds or jet stripes, because that was both correct and precise enough. No mistake on that.

No, what she was thinking of as a slightly erroneous term, or at least misplaced, or hit a little beside what she actually thought was the term 'disfigured'. That the sky was disfigured by the white cloud formations. And that was not what she meant.

That the beautiful blue sky should even be disfigured by the little white cotton wool clouds or even by the jet stripes- that was pure nonsense. Unless you were a completely fanatical believer in everything that was blue, simply because it was blue, and so fierce, you did not tolerate something disturbing the blue. And she was not like that.

On the contrary, she thought it was embellished. That it just made it even more beautiful. Both with the small white cotton wool-like clouds on part of the sky, and also with the long white stripes of the jet exhaust all over the sky. They were actually really nice, she thought. Beautiful, even. Like an ornament.

But her thoughts went astray. She had to acknowledge that. She had to take a roof in herself and get back on track again before it started to run all the way out a tangent that you did not know where to go.

But that was the word. That the small beautiful white summer clouds and the beautiful white jet fighter stripes should have even disfigured the beautiful blue sky. It was pure nonsense and nonsense. She did not think they did at all. On the contrary. It was the exact opposite of what she meant. That on the contrary they decorated, and just made it even more beautiful and more beautiful. So that was a completely wrong word to use about it.

After all, there were so many things that disfigured the world in our day. In many different areas. Unfortunately, she had to acknowledge that. But not just this.

Although she may not have loved those military planes, whether you called them one or the other, she had to admit that the white stripes they made in the sky were beautiful. Decorative.

They gave a kind of contrast to the blue sky. Not a hard contrast. Not like anything that was the direct opposite. But a kind of more gentle contrast that emphasized the beautiful blue sky itself. It kind of put a little emphasis on it, so you really noticed how beautiful it was.

Both the small white clouds that looked like cotton wool and the long white stripes after the jets just make the clear blue sky even more beautiful.

And therefore, the word 'disfigure' is completely wrong. Totally out of place. Not that she was a word fighter. Not very much in any case. If she had to say it, if you just asked her about it, she hated using the words in a way that was a little wrong or incorrect. Or completely wrong. Like this was.

It was, after all, more of an ornament to the blue sky. Something that embellished it. Something that made it prettier. If there was otherwise a word like 'ornamental'. In fact, she did not know if that did. That was it, officially. The spelling dictionary had thus received The Language Board's blue vote and official approval, which one might well use. On the other hand, she was not so sure. In fact, she doubted that was the case directly.

But unfortunately, it was nothing new. She had previously found that both The Language Board and the spelling dictionary did not really follow the way the language actually developed in, but were thoroughly afterwards. Worse, they did not always grasp all the nuances of a word or a way of articulating themselves, which she had been very successful in her years.

Surely there should be a word that meant the opposite of 'disfiguring'. Some of those on The Language Board might argue that you could just use the word 'adorn'. That it graced the blue sky. But it was not a very precise word, not nearly as sharp and precise as 'disfigure'. There was really something slammed in that word, and it was not in a word like 'adorn'. It could not even match up with a word like 'disfigure'. It was not at all lap height. And two words that meant the opposite should be. It was unbelievable that The Language Board could not see it.

But she did not bother to sit down and write another letter about how wrongly The Language Board too often took its job and how much they had misunderstood their taxpayer-funded job. She did not want to. Not until she finished cleaning the house, at least.

These days, with all the modern foreign language that poured across borders like an avalanche of weed seeds, one could never be entirely sure what such people as those who sat on The Language Board could come up with.

She wondered if The Language Board even knew a word like language pollution. Actually, she was not even sure. She wondered if it was in the spelling dictionary. It probably did not. She wouldn't be surprised if it did not. Although, of course, it was perfectly obvious that it should, but things weren't always as they should be. Not even in the language field. Maybe especially there, she knew only too well.

She did not actually own a spelling dictionary herself. She did not see any reason for that. She knew how to spell the words. And if she had such a behemoth of a book in the house, then she would just be driven to look up all sorts of words all the time, just to check if they had now been changed to something strange since then, when she herself went to school and learned to spell.

That was the way it did at the time. Straightening there was a subject called, and it was one of the most important subjects at the time. Since then, it had gone woefully downhill with this kind of thing. I wonder if the schoolchildren of today even knew the word 'spelling'? it could be that it was not in the spelling dictionary anymore! It shouldn't even surprise her. So today you had to use only the word 'spelling', even if it was not nearly as precise.

Today, schoolchildren only learned spelling, not correct spelling. That was a pretty significant difference. If they even learned spelling more, and not just sat in circles and talked in each other's mouths all the time. Back then, when she was at school, it was different. That was when you took going to school seriously. You did not just talk in each other's mouths. At all, you did not talk. People talked. And not in each other's mouths. But politely raised your finger when you wanted to say something, and then you waited nicely for the teacher to allow you to say something. They learned to be quiet instead of making noise and shouting and screaming all the time.

There was actually something called still play. It used it, for example, sometimes when there was a substitute. Then they'd play still games. Which was to sit completely still for as long as possible. And then try to compete with yourself to be completely quiet for a really long time, so you could set a personal record in it, you could almost say.

She wondered if that word even existed. Still play. She wondered if it was in the spelling dictionary anymore. She was pretty sure that is was not. Although it was more necessary now than it had ever been, with all the noise and noise that was exposed everywhere today. There was certainly enough to address before The Language Board. If they had otherwise been their task adult. After all, the spelling dictionary was not worth the paper on which it was printed.

But she still could not fully combat her skepticism about whether the beautiful old words still existed. That is, according to the spelling dictionary. Not just according to common sense, because the two things had little to do with each other. It was very much possible that the word had succumbed to the tooth of the present, as were so many other good, solid and well-used words that should have deserved a better fate. You could never quite know what The Language Board came up with.

These were the strangest words that were declared obsolete by The Language Board and were suddenly stripped of their residence permit in the spelling dictionary. They were crudely and brutally expelled from the language and exiled in a linguistic no-man's land. Deprived of all language rights and public support.

Or no, those were not the words that were strange. It was a bad use of words, it could easily be misunderstood. For example, by The Language Board, which had it with misunderstanding almost everything they came near. The very words that were exiled from the spelling dictionary were not wrong. But the strange thing was that they were taken out of service and sent for scrapping. There was no reason at all. It was almost even weirder than all the new words that The Language Board was so busy cramming into the language all the time. And it was often some really curios words.

She did not know if the word 'ornamental' was in the spelling dictionary. But truth be told, she did not really care. She used it anyway, whether that silly spelling dictionary had it with it or not. It was not exactly what she used as a criterion for her language. It was her own sense of which words were good and suitable and expressed something in a good way, and what words that she just thought sounded totally silly and useless.

The spelling dictionary could not be counted on anymore.

It was her small, sly rebellion against the unfairness of modern society, the decay of seats and all the other injustices in modern society that so many people had to suffer in our day. That was how she perceived it, even if she did not exactly articulate it so accurately.

If she had power and influence, she would start work on a dictionary of good old words from the 1700s and 1800s- and perhaps even further back. In fact, she often read books from the good old days, the classics of literature, and she found that many of these good old words from that time – and the whole language used at the time – were often much more expressive and precise than the modern, pre-interpreted language that modern writers mostly used in our day, and which The Language Board and other similar language depraved did its part to propagate further, rather than stand guard about the good old words, and the good, old, expressive language. It was mainly the individual words she wanted to focus on in this context.

What she wanted was simply to create a dictionary where you could go in and look up one of the modern, gimmicky words or phrases, and then find out what the same word would be called in 18th- or 19th-century language. So one could simply improve one's language or choice of words by translating the modern flat, simplistic pop words into good, old, solid terms of a much greater purity and linguistic quality, as the best language users among our ancestors would have referred to the things in question.

It was primarily the great writers from the past centuries that she was thinking of. They had mastered a much more beautiful, nuanced and expressive language, she thought. And without all these simplistic words and superficial phrases that ravaged the language like a dirty deluge of linguistic sewage sludge.

And what she meant, was not a dictionary where you could look up the old words and have them translated into modern. That kind of thing already existed. No, this was the exact opposite.

So you could translate the modern language that was spoken in this country today into the beautiful, and much more expressive words of the past, so that you could beautify both the spoken and especially the written word, and at the same time contribute to the fact that the good old words for these things did not go into oblivion and disappear, as many of them were unfortunately well on their way to, assiduously helped along the way by The Language Board and the spelling dictionary. She always stressed that strongly when explaining it to someone. And she often had to, because it had become something of a special case for her, and most people did not care much about it.

It might well be that in between there were also some professional terms for modern technical things and things like that, but then you could just use some compositions of the old ore-happy words to describe them with.

Such a dictionary would in itself give a tremendous boost to the linguistic level in this country, she said. This was the kind of thing that The Language Board would have had to deal with if they had otherwise been up to their task and had taken the language problems seriously. But they clearly did not, as she repeatedly patiently explained to those who bothered to listen to it.

But she was still diligent in writing reader letters to the newspapers about it every time there was an opportunity for it in some discussion about the language and the way it was used. She had her point of view and her firm opinion on that matter, and she intended to stick to it.

And then those who cheap and willingly pee in The Language Board for her sake could get

a foal across, while they logged and laughed
with full force for almost every conceivable
form of flattened, gimmicky pop-words,
which piece by piece disfigured the language
more and more.

Cheating with the hearing aid

Summer was still waiting for it, or even just the more serious spring. But it had finally become a slow and hesitant sunny weather. The sun had been slow to come forth and break through the clouds. Even now, it occasionally went behind one of the many small clouds in the otherwise blue sky. It was about to become trivial.

"That was how the weather has been all spring," sighed Vera. But it was not quite right. Because there were also many days when it had been much worse than that, where it had been massively grey weather all day. There had also been quite a few days when the rain had been pouring down. So the weather right now was actually a nice bit above average, although there were many people who had a hard time realizing it, including Vera, who had been married to Brian for so many years. And still it was, despite all their troubles over the years.

But she often felt like she was complaining about the weather. It had almost become a kind of hobby for her, some said. It was kind of negatively worded. And in reality, there are probably not very many people in this country who do not have a strap of skin when it comes to it. It would almost be strange, too, with the weather usually prevailing here at our latitudes.

She might have just put it a little more into the system than most of the rest of us. She saw all the weather forecasts on TV. And those on the web too, of course. And then she discussed them wildly and furiously with Brian. Admittedly, he did not care much about that. Or, of course, he did, but not as much as her. Yet he was gentlemanly enough to discuss this and other similar issues with his dear wife. He may have almost thought it was part of his marital duties.

It was not because he always behaved like the perfect gentleman, but right in this area he actually did it. It was perhaps also a fairly easy area to do it in. And then he might feel like he had fulfilled part of his quorum - what that kind of thing was about.

But in the family there were others, including Jeanette, whom I have mentioned before, but also several others, who felt that it was probably more because he was something of a slipper hero who could not pull himself together to put his foot down and speak out in the face of her perpetual discussions about the weather and weather forecasts.

In fact, she also tormented many other family members as soon as there were a few of them gathered for a larger or smaller gathering of some kind. But many of us were not nearly as patient with what Brian apparently was for the most part.

She is regularly rather offended by that.

Perhaps because she was better used from home, and therefore expected the same from everyone else. But it just was not like that. Then she came across the cuffs, as they say, and pulled out the sensing horns, at least for a while, and often sat and sulked. But it also meant that when she got home, she had even more accumulated weather talk, which she had to drain for towards Brian. But he used to take it with exalted calm, as I understand it. He was used to it.

There were some of the other married women in the family who sighed longingly at the thought of such a patient and understanding husband, who evidently continued to bother to add to all her regrets and the sheer nonsense she sometimes fired off.

They knew that these types of husbands can be hard to drive up, and that their own man at home could not really stand the distance as to what that kind of thing was about. The men usually grumble a little more about it.

"I can't believe he's going to put up with it,"
they muttered, but mostly when their wives
or girlfriends did not listen.

That was how it went for a long time. In fact,
right up until that, it was discovered by a
pure coincidence that Brian was suffering
from a rather solid hearing damage, which he
had, however, for many years gone and kept
secret. But not because he did not care or
because he just ignored it. At the same time,
he had acquired a rather advanced and,
above all, very small and almost invisible
hearing aid that had been camouflaged so
well that it was very difficult to detect if he
did not know it was there.

Apparently, he had rehearsed himself in some
special ways of dealing with it. For example,
he could turn on the hearing aid, quite
discreetly and without her noticing- when
there was a football game on TV, or another
broadcast that he wanted to watch, or when
he was with friends. Or at a family party. But
just as discreetly, he was able to turn it off

again without her suspicions when she embarked on one of her long-running outpourings about the weather and not least the different weather forecasts.

It was probably just the explanation for his great patience with all her regrets and, both in this area and in a number of other fields. It was not really like that at all, because he was not the patience himself, or any particular gentleman. It was just that he – literally – let all her opinions go in one ear and out the other.

A lot of people thought it was cheating. Pure cheating. They did not think it was a smart idea he had had at all. They thought he jumped over where the yeast was lowest and let it go too easily, not least Vera herself when she finally discovered it after he had been running it that way for several years. She was furious.

She really thought he had cheated. I think she felt almost deceived, deceived simply. Almost like if he had cheated on her. Of course, he sometimes did, but probably most in the small things department, as Uncle Jim used to call it, much to the outrage of most of the family's female members.

But apparently Vera had not discovered that yet. It certainly did not work like that. So for the time being she was just seriously angry with him about it with his secret hearing aid and his annoying habit of just turning her opinions on and off, her admonitions and all her many other views on this or that as it suited him.

The result was that in the future she felt compelled to carefully check when he turned on and off that hearing aid. So now there was no longer anything with him being able to just turn it off when, for example, she complained about the weather and the miserable weather forecasts. Just to mention that example.

At first, Brian apparently felt that he had to make good mines for the game and continue to pretend with great patience he was listening to it all, thus maintaining the illusion that he was a patient and understanding gentleman- such a kind ofsuper-husband of the kind that probably doesn't exist in reality.

But, of course, it did not last long. So it was not long before he fell out of the role, now that he could not just turn it off, and then I have to promise that he started contradicting her at one point after another. Not only about the weather, but also all sorts of other things. For a long period of time, it led to countless violent quarrels between them.

It was terrible to listen to them during that time, because they did not stay too good at arguing, so it rattled, even though there were others who listened to it, and often about the pure trifles. I think it went almost to the point where their marriage was cracking. They could soon celebrate the silver wedding and had shown until then a fairly well-functioning marriage, the circumstances taken into account.

But many of us were worried that there would be a silver wedding at all, or if they would split up even before then. It's really weird, but there's often been almost a kind of tradition in our family. That a long-standing marriage cracks and falls apart either just before or just after the two parties involved have fought their way up to the silver wedding.

The one who supports them both

It was still grey weather. Or, to put it quite correctly, now it was graying again. Because there had actually been a few days of some sunshine sometimes. But it almost came out on one. It was like one long grey day, they were spring - they both seemed. In fact, they fully agreed on that.

Yes, that was how it was, Thought Brian. That was how it felt. Almost like an autumn day. Or maybe as a clouded April day with weather that switched between grey weather and rain showers and a little sunflower and cloudy and wind and rain and all over again. So what was it most reminiscent of? Autumn weather? Or April weather?

He could not really decide what to compare it to. April weather would, of course, be better suited to the time of year it actually was, but the weather itself did not get any better. He did not really care what the correct name was. For his sake, you could call it what you wanted. He was just unhappy with the weather as it was, that was all. And really good old fashioned inspiring and rousing spring weather certainly was not. At least that much was clear. And Vera was absolutely right in this, he thought, which was not always a matter of course.

He was not into the long explanations or the complex speculation about it. But then it was good that he had his faithful wife, Vera. For once, they were almost more than entirely in agreement. It must be a variant of that, with external adversity creating inner unity. They were at least unusually in agreement. At least right on that point. And for a long time, several weeks, actually, almost without interruption.

Several of us noticed. Even the hearing aid seemed to have slipped a little in the background. It was already a year ago. It was great to see that they were obviously getting a bit more together again. Then maybe there was hope that their silver wedding would come to something. A lot of us were looking forward to it. It was almost several years ago that there had been a really big family party of this type.

Vera was originally from Norway. But when she was in her mid-twenties, she went to Denmark and stayed here. Even married, later on. Why don't I know. It was probably something about her wanting to study in Copenhagen or something. But I don't think that she completed her studies. But on the other hand, I don't know much about her youth. Only what she's told, and it's not very much. But she sometimes longed for the happy blossoming youth days she had had in Norway before she went down here. I know that. And met Brian, her husband, after first layering with a few others on a slightly more loose basis, and went around and made a bit of each.

Not least with her best friend back then, Bettina. I wonder what had actually happened to her. I wonder if they are still in contact. I do not think so. She never talked about her anyway. That was so many years ago. And I don't think it ended very well what they did together. But I think it was only a couple of years when she was very young. Before she got to know Brian and calmed down a little more. Settled down with and family and children and all that kind of things.

They got married a few years later, but i do not think there was any question of settling in Norway. Not by what I know anyway. I do not know everything they have discussed internally, especially when they were young and newlyweds, because that time I did not even know them yet. But they stayed down here in Denmark.

They had lived in several different places. At first they had probably moved around a bit, but for the past several years they had lived in the small detached house, which was a little secluded on a rather quiet residential road on the outskirts of Copenhagen. After all, there is no need to clarify it any more than that.

At this time, they actually had two adult children, but they had both chosen to settle abroad and resume contact with their Norwegian roots in the grandparents' generation, and their Norwegian cousins. I think there was a lot for them. So it was not so much that Vera and Brian saw for their children and grandchildren.

Incidentally, Brian was only the father of one of their two adult children, the youngest named Susanne. The eldest, named Morten, was born a few years before he got to know Vera. And Susanne only 4-5 months after their wedding. So I think that was almost why they finally married, having been dating for at least a few years and several times having been close to splitting up. At least there were quite a few stories about that. And

I don't think it was just low-lying lies and backless rumors all.

Or – I kind of wonder. I think it was three children they had? All long ago grown up and moved away from home of course. There was also - what was his name? - Yes, Kenneth, his name was. After all, he lived over there in the United States, where I think he had come over as an exchange student originally.

And then he had stuck over there, even though I did not really think you could just do it like that. But I think that was right. I almost forgot about him. I've never met him myself, even though I've come with them quite a bit, and I think he was the eldest of the three children. But has it been Brian's who he has brought with him from a previous relationship? Before he met Vera? Actually, I don't know. But it could almost indicate that.

But either way, they had at least stayed here, in this country - that is, Vera and Brian. Maybe because Brian had his good well-paid job here. That kind of thing can be pretty crucial. He was a driving manager at a large haulage company. He had now reached an age when he might well have retired, but he was one of those who preferred to keep working.

One of the hardworking men, that holds society together. That is the way he sees himself, I think. But in reality, he probably had several different reasons for it. But it would be a little strange to them that all their three children live abroad so that they do not see much of them. They are probably missing them quite a lot. I'm pretty sure of that.

But especially in relation to this weather, she actually had a pretty harsh kind of relationship with it. Maybe because the weather down here in Denmark is a lot different from where she had grown up. And the nature and everything. The geography.

She came from a slightly smaller town far up in Norway. Maybe not exactly Northern Norway, but certainly not down there in southern Norway around the Oslo fjord. Well up. I think it was a town a little north of Trondheim, as Far as I remember. About that, at least. I don't remember what the city's name is, but it's not that important either. A rather small town, anyway.

But it was certainly a place where the weather was a lot different than down here on Zealand. That was probably what was crucial, and that was why she was so aware of all that about the weather. Whereas Brian, who was raised in Nørrebro or Vesterbro or wherever it was, at least somewhere inside Copenhagen, what is usually called the real Copenhagen with big K, the central Copenhagen, he did not care nearly as much about all that sort of thing.

In a different way than her at least. And you can understand that, too. No, I think it was on Østerbro that he grew up. Most of the time at least. On outer Østerbro. Or no, there on the border between Østerbro and Nørrebro. That was where he grew up, I think. But of course it has not so much to do with the weather, where in Copenhagen he just grew up.

As long as he had his new flat-screen high definition TV set with a 60-inch screen and a good football game to watch, or some other kind of sport, and a frame of beer – whether it was big or small lagers, as he called it – he was a happy man. Mostly at least. And all his betting systems, and those other games that had something to do with sports.

Well, he may never have had one of the huge gains, not at least what I know of, but over the years it has dripped a great deal with both small and some quite medium-sized gains. And it usually been celebrated along with friends, or some of them at least. I've been to the house a few times myself. And then he can be quite generous with both. Well, I think I'm going to make sure I don't get on slippery ice.

That was what happened to the wife I came from. His wife's name is Vera, which I've already mentioned. In a way it was probably very nice for her, kind of easy and convenient that he was so preoccupied with all that football and sports and TV. Although she might think it got a little too much sometimes.

That it almost took the upper hand. And I guess it did, too. Especially when there were those big tournaments- which he went into, but otherwise it was very nice for her that it did not take any more to make him happy. When you consider how many angry and disgruntled husbands there are in this world.

And then it kept him at home behind the four walls of the home, as they say, instead of running around town and scoring loose ladies he could have liked. That sounds pretty likely. I certainly know that. But I think it's very common, especially when they're not quite young anymore.

The Book-lover

And now I am going to tell you some more about Vera. She is concerned about all this. The problem is that she has a slightly ambiguous relationship with his interest in football and all that. But it's probably become a little more pronounced over the years as he goes more and more into all that thing with football and sport.

I mean, only watching it on TV. It's not something he cultivates himself, that was how active. He doesn't have time at all, he usually says, because then he can't watch all the football and other sports on TV that he had like to follow. He has, of course, made sure that they have the big channel package, or whatever it is, he calls it, the one with all the sports channels. It almost goes without saying when he's so much into something like that.

But as far as Vera is concerned. On the one hand, it's very nice for her that he has a job to do, so he's mostly on the couch when he has done the day's work in that job he's got in a haulage company.. And that he invites friends to his house instead of running around to those out in the city. Or no, he's stopped on the job, isn't he? Yes, I think so. That was already a few years ago. I don't see them quite so much anymore.

The thing about sports and football on TV, it must give her some reassurance that he is certainly not doing the wild and violent displays. Although it can sometimes be going on when she is not at home, because she has to visit a friend, or if she goes to some evening school or something. She does that sometimes, but it's not often. Or it's shown mostly in winter at least.

For the most part, she's home in the evenings and on weekends, so she can keep a little leash that he doesn't make too much of a. I think she almost thinks that all this kind of thing is a thing of the past for him. It's just too much shame, I mean, that it's going to happen with a little too much shame. So I'm not going to cut shards by being too open-mouthed. There is no reason to put their marriage in jeopardy here just before the silver wedding, so we also miss that party, just as happened to Birgit and Paul a few years ago.

They broke up with legal divorce and all the squeaky, bad things and every imaginable sympathy in the back order only 6 months before their silver wedding, because there was someone who had been too open-mouthed about something that one of them had been up to, or it was actually both of them. So around different places of course.

But there is no reason for that. It's just too silly. Then we missed that party, too. It's boring, many almost-silver wedding couples have gotten over the years, I think. They could just when the silver wedding was brought in before they break apart. That must be the minimum when they're so close.

Even if they now hate each other a great deal, whether they now have reason to do so or not and certainly have no plans to stay together forever.

But that was not really what I wanted to tell you. It is because in many ways she has a little different interests than those he cares about so much. But I guess that was the way it is.

But to give a rather important example, it has turned out that Vera suffers from an unrequited love of books and literature and things like that with philosophy and all the kind of thinking a little more about life. And you know what that kind of thing can lead to. On top of that, she herself has an unrealistic urge to philosophize about things herself. She openly admits that.

But maybe she's also a little influenced by her profession. Or quite a lot actually. People get that a lot. I know many examples of this. In fact, both good and bad, if I'm going to be a little objective.

But the fact of the matter is that she has been employed as a librarian at the local municipal library for many years. That was all very well, especially if she had stopped in time and retired, as planned, instead of continuing at half-time. That was where the chain jumped off. Actually, it was.

After all, she would have liked to have discussed what she was reading, and also her own excursions into the nooks and crannies of her mind with her husband. But that kind of interested person isn't really Brian. It was her great sadness that it was not possible. She's said that a lot. Many times. And just with the expression that it was her great sadness that she could not discuss things like that with Brian. I tend to think that was right enough.

That was probably why she definitely wanted to continue working half-time at the library. I think so. Then she could at least discuss it with her colleagues over there. For most of them, they were also very interested in books and all that. Although of course it also had a job they had to look after, so they could not just sit and discuss literature all day. Especially not after the recent cuts. But a little bit, maybe there might be time for some time.

But then it was that it happened. For a younger male librarian had just been hired at the small local library where she was employed. He was about the forty, I think, at least a few years younger than her. And he had a great interest in most of the same writers and the same philosophers with whom she was so preoccupied. It could almost only go wrong. He was even divorced. Newly divorced. Less than six months ago.

So it went as it had to go. Before long, they were complicated by long philosophical and literary discussions every day during the lunch break. Soon they started to take a break in the local café every afternoon after the end of the work. Not to flirt or to cheat on anyone. But only to continue their deep and obviously very intense discussions about books and literature and writers and philosophy.

In fact, it went well for a long time. But then it was that she got the ill-thought that she would start working full-time again. No doubt with the hidden agenda and the secret purpose that there was then an opportunity to spend even more inspiring and intellectually stimulating hours with his library heritage. And then, of course, Brian at home began to wonder.

Because he had a good salary where he worked, so there was plenty for both of them with what he earned. He had already told her more than once that she did not have to go to work because he earned everything they needed. So she could retire. They could do without her pay, he said.

I do not know whether she directly argued with women's rights to make their own money and not to be dependent on a man who could support them. But she certainly did not bow to his attempts to keep her at home with her meat pots, frying pans and his new dish.

Because that, of course, was Brian's real intention. Keeping her at home all the time so she had a lot more time to go and socialize with him and make more of the household and the cooking, and all that domestic stuff that he thought she was starting to slop a little with here lately. Whether it was right or not. But at least she said stop.

I think it almost made her more stubborn and more determined to keep her job at the library at almost any cost. She could be like that sometimes. She insisted. And even taking some extra hours so she actually got back up to full-time. Once she had put something in her head, she did not give it up so easily again.

She was not completely lost in the back of a wagon, so she quickly turned her attention to the fact that it was a question of equality and women's politics and all the kind that used to put him a little to the wall. For all his other vices notwithstanding, however, he had finally followed so much over time that he did not like to be seen as an old-fashioned house tyrant and male chauvinist who oppressed women.

So it happened that Vera gave back with just about the same coin one day when they sat at dinner. She suggested that he might as well stop working when she went full-time. Brian was about to lose both the knife and the fork when she said it, but she had been counting on it, and had come to the conclusion that, although her full-time salary was not as high as his, they could still make their finances work when they took his pension savings into account and if he then got early retirement, which he was still entitled to. And why shouldn't the woman as well be the one who supported them both, as the man, she asked.

After all, he could not really give that back on without revealing himself as the oppressor of women; he was probably still a bit of deep down, despite all his attempts to keep up with the times and try to understand the trends that were moving in it. So then he was almost speechless.

So now she knew how to argue her case. So she went on to say that if he stopped working and let her make a profit, he could also take over all the household work and cleaning and cooking and laundry and all that stuff when he had to go home all day while she was at work anyway. That was when he became even more speechless. He never imagined that.

The idea that they could do without his masculine income was bad enough in itself. But the fact that he was also going to run around at home with an apron on and cook and clean and wash clothes while she was at work was just about to tear the rug away from under him. But as Vera so narrowly put it: now for decades she had been in charge of all those things while doing her job as a librarian, most of the years until recently even full-time.

So why wouldn't he be able to handle it when he was just walking at home all day, she asked. Then it wouldn't really be fair to swap a little bit about the roles now. Maybe he did not think that sounded pretty reasonable? And had he ever had anything to complain about in connection with her housekeeping?

Brian tried to argue about this question, but he probably should have done it. What he made was an exceptionally bad argument. He was stupid enough to mention it with her cooking in the first year of their marriage. Back then, she had not been very good at cooking. Pretty miserable, actually.

What he had complained about at the time was that his mother had finally taken action and taken his newlywed daughter-in-law to school. Back then, Vera had been much quieter and restrained than it is now. And perhaps she had managed to believe that it was a special kind of family tradition. Something that was quite common.

In any case, it had become that a young newlywed couple would show up at their mother-in-law's every weekday when they came from work, and then the mother-in-law otherwise started a quite hard core cooking class for the son's newlywed wife, with special emphasis on his son's favorite foods and his penchant for thick brown sauce.

During a winter, Vera had become an almost perfect cook, at least on Brian's favorite dishes, but the humiliation of being taken to school by the tough mother-in-law who did not think she did well enough for her son, she never forgot.

That is why, of course, it was a major misstep on his part to bring this very matter forward. It really made him sound like a genuine old-fashioned male chauvinist and an ungrateful and demanding old-fashioned husband who almost regards his wife as some kind of slightly more upgraded maid or housekeeper.

It quickly dawned on him, almost immediately after the words had come out of his mouth. It was such an under-the-question argument that he alone had lost the discussion, and then he clapped like an oyster and let his wife work as much as she wanted, without further questions or comments. So she had the opportunity to enjoy the wonderful conversations about profound philosophical questions and literary interpretations along with her increasingly dear library heritage, about which Brian fortunately knew nothing.

The new tradition

Vera looked out the window. She just had to check to see if the weather had improved. It had not. It looked grim. The clouds and stuff. Dark in the weather it was too. It often is when it's really massively cloudy. It looked pretty sad. Not exactly encouraging in any case.

I don't think the weather really could decide what it would. This morning, when she got up, it was sunny weather. Well, it actually had. It just did not last very long. As early as early in the morning, the clouds began to pull together. Now they covered almost all of the sky.

Once in a while, the sun looked out from behind a cloud, just for the sake of sight, it almost seemed like. Just for a moment. After a few minutes, it disappeared again behind the clouds. That is, a different cloud. Not just the same as before. That was how it was that day. The clouds could not stay calm either. Very changing. A little bit one and a little the other. As if it could not decide whether it would one way or the other. She knew that from herself. But still. That was why the weather did not have to overdo it quite so much. We know that from ourselves. That was it, it's going to be really bad. When it collapses like that.

But she was actually trying to take it away from the positive side. She did. At least it did not look like rain. Not for the time being. It was not that kind of cloud. After all, they did not look like that either. It was just some nice, bright clouds, even though they covered the whole sky. Not such heavy gray rain clouds. Not very much gray. Hardly at all. It was not that worse. She could clearly see that now.

She started making afternoon coffee and bread. The question was where to drink their afternoon coffee today. It was getting warm enough in the weather for them to be outside in the garden. If only it would not happen to start raining while they sat out in the garden and enjoyed their coffee. Brian, of course, had not finished the conservatory. It would otherwise have been convenient to have in a situation like this.

But that was the way it was with Brian. Too often. Sometimes he could be incredibly long on things. Especially if it was something that did not really interest him. And conservatories weren't exactly his strong side or what he cared about most, especially when he had to make them himself. It was not even done half-finished yet. The conservatory was even worse.

So it might be useful to rely on it. And now she had to make a decision soon. She thought about it. It was important to her that they took the coffee out in the garden. That was what she wanted most. In fact, they had already started on that in the hot period a few weeks ago. But then there had been a week of cool and windy weather. Now is the time to resume that tradition. The new tradition that she had created, or recreated, here in the dawning but also slightly belated spring.

It was important for her to keep it in contention. It was to become their lovely summer tradition. It would be of no use if it started to crumble even now. It was now for her to insist on it and insist that this is how it should be.

Traditions were important. She had learned that from home. It was also important to create one's own personal traditions, to complement the inherited family traditions. It was the kind of thing that created order and system in life.

Not only by the big part, but also in the small. Traditions of daily life. Not just for the holidays. Give us today our many small, daily traditions, just as we also count on others to respect their traditions and the ways they usually do things.

That was how you could almost put it.

Some might rather just call it habits. Or routines. Or maybe even habits. She knew that kind of thing. These were the kind of people who did not really take things seriously. Habits. Routines. She tasted the words. It sounded so boring. So gray and sad. It sounded like a bit of treadmill. It sounded very negative, it actually sounded way too much like the old treadmill, she thought.

Then it almost sounded as if you had grown into routines that you were not in control of, or which you perhaps even felt like a victim of. Or even WAS the victim of. That was kind of way too passive. It was one of the worst things she knew. She wanted to avoid that for everyone. It was absolutely nothing to aspire to.

Or was it something like her sister, who always talked about "bad habits." Oh no, it was not a nice swung word. And not just over the word itself. But over the whole concept. And over the practice that was attached to observe the traditions, both in everyday life and even more the holidays and other more special occasions.

So she agreed with herself that this new tradition, it had to be maintained, so that it could become a really solid established tradition. Because at this point it was really only a tradition, you could say. A tradition of creation.

A new tradition that had to be cared for and nursed and nursed so that it could enter into character in earnest. So that it could have the time and strength to establish itself as one of those traditions that was so solid and entrenched and which was regarded as so obvious, that they were automatically observed, almost as by themselves. She had decided.

This was supposed to be one of the real good new traditions- which continued almost by itself once it was established. At the same time, it was also a somewhat exciting experiment to practice before creating and establishing the really serious traditions of the future part of their marriage, which in some respects needed an overhaul if it were to be able to continue in a slightly better and more satisfying way than the slightly creaking wobbly back and forth and from side to side, which in truth had marked it a little abundantly in recent years.

Now it was time to tighten up and put some new and better buns on the soup. Even Brian had to understand that. And this first of the new traditions was at least so harmless that he could hardly be familiar with having any aversion to it.

And at the same time, it could nonetheless help to enshrine the principle that new and perhaps slightly different traditions were needed in their continued cohabitation. For that, he probably just had to get used to that - as solid as he had become with the old and slightly devoured ways of doing things. So now we needed some renewal, she thought.

Springtime dinner

Vera got up and went into the kitchen to put the potatoes over. It was the expensive organic ones. It should be a proper quality. She almost always cooked potatoes for dinner. Almost whatever it was they were supposed to have for dinner that day. It had almost become a regular routine with her.

This was, of course, due to the fact that she mostly made dinner dishes that were suitable for being served with potatoes as an accessory. Such an old-fashioned dinner dishes, many would probably call it.

However, although she referred to the potatoes as an accessory to the meat dish and the possible vegetables, which also often belonged, it was in fact the potatoes that made up the bulk of what was on the dishes and plates. At that point, she was probably pretty old-fashioned, too.

A dish of dinner, which was not mainly made up of potatoes, was for her no real dinner. Not a perfectly good and sensible form of dinner in any case.

It was also the reason why she never, so to speak, or in each only extremely rarely, served tomato sauce. In her firm and persistent opinion, tomato sauce did not really belong to proper and sensible dinner dishes. In her opinion, tomatoes were a part of the cold kitchen. That is, it was lunch, not dinner.

Not hot food. Tomatoes could be excellent on an egg meal, or as cold cuts in the form of mackerel in tomato. Or as tomato boats along with cucumber slices in a bowl of green salad. That kind of thing. She could accept that. Maybe a little tomato slices too. But it was also about that, she preferred long raw tomatoes. All those modern kinds of spaghetti sauce and pesto and all that stuff she had not really reached yet.

Tomatoes did not have a very high star with her. She used everything to highlight as an argument that tomatoes could not be grown in this country in the open air. Not commercially, anyway. In this country they were grown in large greenhouses that swallowed a lot of energy for heating.

Or they had to be grown under more southern climes, where it was warmer and more sunlit, and then they were flown here by air freight, which also required a lot of energy and thus was to the detriment of the environment. Therefore, tomatoes should not have a prominent role in good Danish cooking, she said.

When they did not naturally belong in the climate we had at these latitudes, they did not belong on the Danish dinner tables either. That was her point of view. She cared about that.

But she also had other arguments. For example, she thought it would be a kind of double confection if you served potatoes and tomatoes together. They were too closely related, she said. Kind of cousin-like. Although of course they tasted quite different and one was a root fruit and the other was a flower fruit. And not a vegetable at all, as most people wrongly called them. A complete misunderstanding, she thought.

She would rather not serve anything that was against the supremacy of potatoes at the dinner table. So bombastic she could almost have even eaten it when she had drunk more than the three usual glasses of red wine with the food – and then maybe a glass of brandy or two for the coffee afterwards.

But at lunch, she did not drink wine. Brian usually drank one or two beers.

In many ways she was a little old-fashioned, some of the slightly younger ones in the family thought, but she did not let herself be challenged by that. She stubbornly stuck to the good old principle that she had learned from her mother and grandmother, and that it was the potatoes that were to be the good, solid base and main ingredient in any sensible dinner. At least in this country. What people came up with of food habits in other countries, they had to lie down and mess with themselves.

In her view, it was in fact the meat that was a kind of modest accessory for the potatoes and not the other way around. Although most were used to highlighting the meat as the most important.

Today we are going to have meatballs for dinner, or sausages, or chops, or tenderloin – or whatever it might be. That was how most people mentioned it, but it was not correct at all, she said. At least not when it came to the food that was served there in the house. She'll take care of that. She could be pretty stubborn with that. Brian, on the other hand, was not. He did not care about anything like that at all. At that point, he was far more modern than her. He would definitely have preferred if it was the meat that was most of the daily dinner, and the potatoes then were only a more modest accessory.

Nor did he have any trace of dislike against tomato sauce or pizza or lasagna or all the kind of newfangled dishes with which she was, in his opinion, overly restrictive. He was also far more fond of good, old-fashioned thick sauce than she was. There is no reason whatsoever that they should have the same kind of taste for all these things.

And Vera definitely held on to hers. Brian's increasingly frequent complaining about it only made her even more stubborn, for she knew that she stood for the good, old sensible and healthy principle, and Brian for unhealthy and frivolous food habits.

She still practiced it in the same way she had learned from her mother and grandmother as a child. That is, one or two meatballs for each – if that is what was on the menu – and then you had to eat potatoes for the rest. That was her principle, and she stuck to it. To Brian's growing irritation.

But she simply saw this as an invitation to repeat her little lecture on the healthier and more sensible food habits of the past.

Because back then, when everyone ate according to these good old fashioned principles, people were not as obese and overweight as they were today, she always stressed that. Hardly anyone was severely obese in the good old days. It was only a few of the rich, usually men, those who were sometimes called dining masters.

Moreover, it was also much more responsible for the environment and climate if we were mainly eating potatoes and other plant products, supplemented by a small amount of meat, rather than vice versa. That was mostly the argument she used.

While most of her other arguments for a more potato-based diet were allowed to take a well-deserved rest break. Without, however, she had even forgotten them or put them on the shelf for that reason. But now it was almost always the one with regard to the climate and the environment that she was driving forward with.

We were pleased about that, because all her many different arguments made us so tired. We had heard it all before, many times. She had repeated them over and over again, especially all those who were about the old days and how much and healthier and better and what-not everything was back then. What on earth would we use it for? Did she imagine that we should just turn back the clock to her great-grandmother's time, or what?

On the other hand, there was also a downside to her new and updated argument. First, she had suddenly become super-modern with that argument. And brought to the forefront of what was seen as good and right and progressive and responsible and all that sort of thing these days. That in itself was a bit of a surprise to us. We wouldn't have been used to seeing her like that. But okay, that was the way it was, and we had to bend over.

Secondly, however, the difference was also that it has a new argument with regard to the environment and the climate, which we could not simply reject that. We had to bend over to that. It belonged to the kind of arguments against which it is very difficult to argue without even appearing like a really stupid pig and a giant egotist. So we just had to bow to that every time we were invited to dinner with her and with Brian.

But we had been in the past, when they were still discussing the other arguments she was running. All those with the old days and so on. They were, of course, easier to argue against, but the reality was that we had to bow to them in practice anyway. In terms of what we got to eat. Because there was never very much on the dishes, especially the dishes with the meat, of course. Potatoes were always there in excessive numbers, it almost goes without saying with the attitude she had to it.

Brian was always sulking about the state of affairs, that was clear.

It also often happened that he spoke with a raised voice and honed arguments. At least he thought it was, but it quickly turned out that they did not last half an inch once he had presented them to Vera. He probably figured that it would help the cause when there were now audiences, namely us, and probably figured that we would be some kind of co-conspirators on his arguments, which we then also tried several times, in each of us, but it just did not really matter anyway.

All his arguments fell rumbling to the ground like overweight turkeys without a parachute, as one of us once put it. So at that point there was not really anything to do. Or we were almost aware of it in advance. Based on the general debate about it. In the media and stuff. Moreover, several of us had actually started to subscribe to the same meatless views themselves. A few had even started to become vegetarians and did not touch anything at all that had to do with meat or other animal products. There were also two who called themselves flexitarians. These are the kind of people who aren't 100 percent vegetarians all the time. Only at home with himself. But they can eat some meat when they're invited to dinner with someone.

But one of the things that has probably puzzled many people other than us was her relationship with vegetables. You'd think she had have been really excited about them. But she just was not. Contrary. And it's a surprise when she was on the very latest fashion trends in terms of eating much less meat. But that was the way it was.

In a way, there was actually a fairly simple and logical explanation for it, that is, from the point-of-view. Because she felt that all the different kinds of vegetables that had gradually come on to the market were competing a little too fiercely with the good old potatoes for the food eaters' favor.

She made no secret of the fact that she had been subjected several times to rude and rude diners who largely left the potatoes untouched back in the bulging potato bowls, while eagerly and energetically taking care of the dishes with vegetables when she was still serving them in a rather more generous way. She simply kept up with the vegetables really violently- forcing them to eat their feet in potatoes if they did not want to go hungry.

Some people thought she exaggerated it a little bit. Or, in fact, a huge amount. Too much. But the fact is that from that time she served only extremely rarely vegetables for hot food. Except for a large bowl of green salad with a little cucumber slices and thin tomato slices sprinkled on top. Always super thinly sliced, both the tomatoes and also the cucumbers. But no cooked vegetables anyway. And certainly not when there were guests. She probably had something to do with the fact that she wanted to raise people a little bit. Definitely.

His attitude to vegetables was kind of more la-la. He was not particularly green-lit. On the other hand, he did not mind them either. He did not have any hang-ups on them, as some men have. He could easily eat them without being encouraged to do so, and even often with something that looked like a kind of enthusiasm, it seems. But it was perhaps mostly because of the lack of meat. So there was a bit of variation in it, and a bit of confusion compared to the potatoes. It could be. At least several of us thought so.

Of course, she also had a fairly extensive set of arguments against vegetables. Or against excessive eating of them, at least. What she called excessive eating of them. One of her main arguments was usually that she simply thought it was uncooperative towards the good old well-earned potatoes that had been ours – not outright us, but the main eatery and firm food sticking point for centuries, that we suddenly let them down and moved on to the much more exciting and varied and exotic vegetables of a thousand different kinds - just because it had now become possible in the shops.

Such a la "the potatoes have done their duty – out to the right with them". Without them being valued on merit. That was what her criticism went on. If you have to sum it up a little. Perhaps she even thought they should be honored with a medal for their efforts to provide food for the people of the country sometime a hundred years ago. Something like that. Or the medal would probably be that we kept eating them every day. As such a kind of twisted accolade, or something like that. But what on earth would that do good for? Sometimes she's just a little too crazy.

Such a really old-fashioned potato mom, as one of us calls it. Someone who also says "Now you're going to eat up!," "You can at least taste it" or "Don't take more to the plate than you're sure you can eat." That type. One of the kind that might give the grandchildren one of the very small soft drinks - for sharing, instead of giving them one of the bigger and more normal ones each.

But here she had found a case in which there were also a number of arguments, which she also repeated as soon as there was the slightest reason for it. She simply thought it was unfair and unfair to the poor solid, sensible and more earthbound and good, old, etc. Potatoes that they were now subjected to comparisons with all the more special and exotic vegetables that were gradually flown in from the other side of the globe in time and prematurely, and for which so many of her acquaintances lay on her stomach.

And that burdened the environment with aviation fuel. She would rather spend the fuel that was now available on transporting people than on flying fruit and veg and other consumables halfway around the globe to the pampered luxury stomachs of rich countries. That was kind of how she put it.

But she also had other arguments. Everything else would have looked bad for her, too. She had always made an argument when you thought that now she had been through the whole row. She also claimed that potatoes are one of the most complete nutrients available.

So when you had the good old potatoes that were so perfect in themselves, it was not necessary – well, almost completely illogical and inherently contentious, as well as a waste of time and etc. – to supplement them with all sorts of other fervently superfluous vegetables of much less nutritional value just for the sake of entertainment, as she called it.

Of course, she also failed to highlight the particularly grim examples, such as avocados, which required huge quantities of water during cultivation and which, therefore, in many of the poor countries where they were grown for export, caused major problems for the more local-oriented agriculture and the local population, especially in the very many places where there were already problems in obtaining enough water. At times, she even called this kind of thing a remnant of the imperialism of the rich, Western world towards poor countries.

Those were just some of her arguments. But the result had been that in hers – and Brian's – home almost without exception, only copious amounts of potatoes were served, A small amount of meat, as well as large and increasing amounts of gravy to get the many potatoes to slip down with us who came to visit and were not used to eating us saturated in the potatoes and therefore needed some dipping (as she pejoratively called it) to get a fairly successful result out of what was, after all, the point of the meal, namely to become saturated.

The same was true of Brian, who was in a similar situation to us, just on a daily basis. Although he actually pretty much mostly carried his fate with patience and without bunion much, at least not when we were there.

As far as is known, he was never allowed to cook for himself. At least that was the impression we got. Because if he first started to be active in the kitchen, it almost invariably resulted in too much meat coming on the plates and correspondingly too few potatoes. That was what Vera said. By the way, I don't think he really liked that kitchen.

The times he had tried his way in the kitchen with the hot food, too many vegetables had often arrived on the table. And even of the more exotic, imported kind. Especially when Vera cut back on the money he got to buy food, so that he simply could not afford to do a lot of meat.

It was as if he would at least spice up the meals with some exotic vegetables. It definitely would not have bothered Vera, if it was the meat he had cut down on in favor of some vegetables, it might have gone ahead, but it was the potatoes that he tried to replace with vegetables as much as was now possible on the basis of the money she had given him to buy food for dinner.

From what we have heard from several different sides, which we are about to stop divulging, it was precisely this that was the real reason why he was dropped from the order as a food thief after a few months of initial but rather unsuccessful efforts in this direction.

It is even reported that at the end of his cooking period he was not even allowed to shop for the dinner meals he was supposed to cook on. For exactly that reason.

We've even heard rumors that when he was home alone every Wednesday night, because Vera went to some evening school course in something, he saw his chance to excel in meat and vegetables. These vegetables were reportedly delivered to the door by a near-neighbor woman who lived a little further down the road. First, in raw mode, which was just put in a bag by the kitchen door, when they were sure that Vera had set off for her evening course.

It was both meat, but also many vegetables, of which the near-neighbor herself cultivated many of them in her own garden. However, it was not very long before it developed, so these foods began to be delivered in prepared condition, and even in a very delicious and well-prepared version, where Susanne, as she was called, herself participated in the cooking process.

Since this could well involve some risk of discovering and revealing the traces that the shared meal easily risked leaving behind, these Wednesday dinners were quite quickly moved to Susanne's house a little further along the road, where, incidentally, she lived alone after the divorce from her husband a few years ago, and without any children living at home, who were now all three adults and long since left home. It was simply just much more practical.

Not least because we have also heard that the unfolding of these Wednesday evenings is far from always confined to the culinary. At least not if this is defined in the too narrow sense.

It is probably also these incidents that form the basis of the rather extensive accusations that Vera later made against Brian for systematic adultery of a particularly serious nature. And as he admitted, after a time of dogged denial, but also took the consequences. Although it was probably a slightly different consequence than the ones you would normally have expected. But it is sometimes difficult to fully clear every detail of this kind of thing. So we'd better save that part of the story for another time.

On the whole, it's ended up getting a bit of a mess, I must confess. It has not quite become as we intended. We have written this together. We have been several people engaged in the writing process, so we may not have managed to keep the same tone all the way through. Although at the same time we have also tried to write it almost as a novel, for it we thought that would be the most fun. We actually started on it - because it was supposed to be a kind of shelf for them, that is, to Vera and Brian, of course, for their silver wedding, which is coming in a short time.

If there is going to be a silver wedding. Because that is not sure at all. It may be cancelled. With all the problems that have arisen here lately. But that was why we started it, as a kind of extended party song, you could almost say. A very extended party song in that case. You have to say that. Somehow we got the idea that we would write it as a whole book about them, you know, the kind with a number of small funny stories about their little quirks that each of them has.

Just like you often do in a party song. I mean, of the more personal kind. But it is not so easy at all when it is elaborated as much as here. Some of it might easily sound a little too critical. A little too close maybe. That we're going to smear too much in it in some places maybe.

And it does not get any easier when all these problems have suddenly arisen with them, which, after all, have not quite been between them before, at least not to this extent. Although of course they have also had their tours in the past.

After all, I don't really know. I do hope they can save their marriage of course, at least until sometime after the party - so that it does not sink in. It is such a shame when a long-standing marriage crashes just before the silver wedding party.

And now I have actually wondered whether some of what we have put together here, with the common help, might be offensive to one of them, or maybe even both of them. Maybe we even risk helping to deepen the problems and disagreements that have been going on between them here lately.

So maybe that was exactly what is going to be the turning point for the silver wedding party. Because, of course, that was not the point. On the contrary. So maybe we should wait to finish it until after they have held their silver wedding in good order? Unless, of course, it escalates between them anyway, and that is the way it looks at the moment. Anyway, it's going to be quite exciting to see how it develops between them here in the coming months.

A contradiction in words

It was cloudy. None of them could deny that it was, no matter how much they wanted to. It had even become more so during the afternoon. Vera was pretty sure of that. Brian, on the other hand, was absolutely certain. For most people, it may well seem like a fairly small difference that one of them was "pretty sure" of it and the other party was "absolutely certain" of it.

But the difference was not small. To link to their own language. It was actually in between some of their friends and acquaintances who did when they were having a little fun over some of the funny things they said and did. In all peace and friendship, of course.

Like this, this difference between two slightly different formulations of pretty much the same thing that Vera and Brian could think of quite a lot if they had nothing else to do and both were a little bored. And it happened sometimes. Quite often, actually.

But that very day, it may not have been entirely a matter of disagreement about the correct language. Because it had been cloudy most of the day. Pretty much cloudy. And then, apparently, it had become a little more cloudy during the afternoon. A little bit. Or was it? Had it even become MORE cloudy?

Or had the cloud masses just been moved around a little bit by the wind, so that in some places there was more massive cloud cover, while elsewhere it had developed into a slightly thinner and less massive cloud cover. So the number or amount of clouds or their total density was actually the same as before, but just distributed a little differently on the celestial vault.

It was the kind of thing they could think of a lot of things sometimes. As I said especially if they were bored something so godly. And they did so - for some reason, which I did not really understand - just this summer. So it was often the kind of thing they did when they were bored.

Or when they just needed to disagree and discuss about something, but still could not really think of something serious to argue about. Or if they both like had the nerves on the outside of the clothes, because it had been this weird sultry and depressing summer weather for a long time now. And then it took almost nothing for them to get annoyed and get into a fight and disagree about things that really mattered. Some very small things.

That was the way things were between them, and it had been so for many years. They were immeasurably interested in details and tiny nuances of meaning. Some - and in fact quite a few - even accused them of being much too concerned with all this, both of them even. But most of all Brian. Vera was quite probably a distinctly word fighter, they thought. But Brian was certainly a very, very distinctly word fighter, they said.

And they discussed it themselves. Quite often, even. For they often argued among themselves about which of the two was the biggest and most stubborn and persistent word fighter, and which of them was the smallest and less insistent word fighter. Which means that he was also the most incompetent and actually rather bad word fighter who had not even properly learned this important craft properly.

Because they could disagree on that, too. Was the word fighter's art – that is, being a truly skilled, competent and well-functioning word fighter in fact mostly a piece of craft that could be learned by diligent training – or rather it was a piece of highly intellectual piece of spirit work that was very much based on innate intelligence and installations for abstract and sophisticated thinking.

They also could not really agree on whether it was something good or something bad to be a big or a little word fighter, respectively. In other words, whether being a word fighter was a term of honor or, on the contrary, a criticism bordering on libel.

Apparently, some middle ground was not for them, because no one – or at least no one – the nuance of meaning – or, more importantly, could also be called conceptual characteristics, if only to be challenged, debated and, in particular, considerably more precise – and more importantly – if only anything else, if only to facilitate understanding of the What they were actually discussing.

And in doing so, it helps to provide some kind of justification for – or one could also justify – why it was even important – or perhaps even almost indispensable – to discuss – or perhaps just quietly discuss – this or that.

They had a lot of time to go with as spring time was slowly turning towards summer.

But at their worst – or most pronouncedly– they could not even agree on what they were actually doing. That question in itself could give rise to a great deal of disagreement between them when they were in that mood. And they were very often. Almost all the time.

But how would this concept actually be understood? Was what Vera claimed – at least mostly, and especially when she had difficulty penetrating with her definition of something – the majority of their waking hours, it spent with some form of word fighter and that type of discussion.

Or was it- in fact, as Brian always claimed, only the second biggest activity in their shared life - if everything was figured out, or else they were doing together in a big pile, such in time, measured in hours and minutes, for example.

And this could very well be done in order to clarify this, he believed, while Vera was of the opposite view and with outrage in the voice categorically maintained. That it would be a completely unheard of and unreasonable way of applying these concepts.

To which Brian immediately reiterated that the expression was completely unheard of, since at least it did not belong anywhere, because she had just heard him say it, and then it could not reasonably be described as unheard of. Such petitess could be given a long time to go along.

Of course, they also could not agree on whether the fact that they spent most of their time (if that was the case) either arguing or discussing all these things basically – or at least as a curious verge remark – was a sign of their great intellectual curiosity and sharpness and therefore something good and laudable and somewhat evolving, it should be encouraged and stimulated as much as possible – or whether, on the contrary, it was a sinus and crude attempt to undermine the other's opinions simply to win a discussion (or an argument) in order to confirm its superiority to the other party. And therefor something bad, which was only kept going by the other's totally bad upbringing and totally exaggerated power-grabbing.

Nor could the question of whether one or the other of these explanations could be regarded as either a good and objective justification or, on the contrary, as a completely disingenuous attempt to justify is completely untenable, they could agree. If that was at all a view, and not just a one-sided propaganda feature that could not be taken seriously at all.

What may be surprising is that, year after year, they continued to spend so much time on this callous word-fighter, when they could have spent time on something considerably more exciting instead. Either with others, maybe out in the city, or they could have had their own interesting hobby.

Or they could have made some holiday trips abroad, maybe just to Mallorca or Turkey or one of the Greek islands, if only to escape the grey, cold and dreary weather in winter. After all, they had enough time after they both retired. Or, as Brian always used to put it carefully, they had both chosen to retire voluntarily from the labor market as soon as they were given the opportunity.

However, there was never any question as to why they had been so eager to retire as early as possible. Was it possibly because similar wordy behavior had occurred in their respective workplaces and that this might have made their thoroughly unpopular with their colleagues? Or with their bosses? Strangely, there was never any mention of that. There seemed to be something here that, for a rare occasion, they agreed on.

It was something new that came as a surprise to many of those who knew them, or were the subject of their otherwise perpetual word-fighting. It was especially some of the family's younger members who cultivated this.

It was originally intended to have just an entertaining little secret activity for some kind of inner circle, but it quickly became the case that a disagreement, or rather a deep divide, arose between two groups of those who looked at it a little differently.

At first it was just supposed to be such a small cheerful thing, where we could have had all the peace so much that Vera and Brian themselves were not even aware that these otherwise rather obvious topics had escaped their attention.

But as I said, a wing soon - or perhaps rather a faction - arose among us, not only to sit and enjoy this little piece of secret knowing, As it actually was in a way, but which would definitely take it a step further to throw such one of their overlooked topics of discussion into the heads of the two stacks, for example, in the middle of a geared-out family gathering, thus sparking a hefty word-like mess in a situation where otherwise a fairly calm and peaceful situation had been set up between the two, and I honestly think that was just negative enough.